Fireman Small

Wong Herbert Yee

Houghton Mifflin Company   Boston   1994

Library of Congress Cataloging-in-Publication Data

Yee, Wong Herbert.
Fireman Small / written and illustrated by Wong Herbert Yee.
p.   cm.
Summary: Every time he gets into bed, Fireman Small is called to
rescue some animal in trouble.
ISBN 0-395-68987-2
[1. Fire fighters—Fiction.   2. Animals—Fiction.   3. Stories in
rhyme.]   I. Title.
PZ8.3.Y42Fi   1994   93-31518
[E]—dc20   CIP
                      AC

Printed in the United States of America

WOZ   10   9   8   7   6   5   4   3   2   1

To Judy, Ben, Margaret, Annie, Mary and Ray
For childhood memories shared

In the middle of town, where buildings stand tall
There lives a little man called Fireman Small.
The only firefighter this side of the bay,
Fireman Small works night and day.

He pulls the truck into station number nine,

Walks upstairs one step at a time.

Closes the curtains, gets in bed

And pulls the covers over his head.

RING-A-LING-DING sounds the alarm.
Cat up a tree at Farmer Pig's Farm!
Quickly out of bed he scoots,
Jumps into his pants and boots.
Ready to go, he slides down the pole
Puts on his helmet and coat below.
Sirens sound, lights flashing round
Fireman Small races through town.

"In the Magnolia," squeals Farmer Pig.

Tiny Cat is clinging to a twig.

Neighbors rush to see what's the matter

Fireman Small springs up the ladder.

The bough breaks and Tiny Cat falls . . .

Into the arms of Fireman Small.

Pig and neighbors all shout: *"HOORAY!"*

Fireman Small puts the ladder away.

He pulls back into station number nine,

Walks upstairs one step at a time.

Closes the curtains, gets in bed

And pulls the covers over his head.

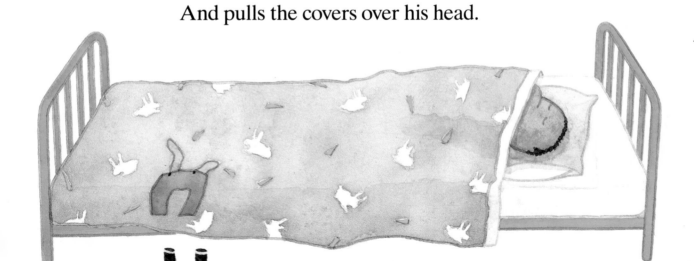

CLING-A-CLING-CLANG rings the bell.

Little Bunny has fallen down the well!

Quickly out of bed he scoots,

Jumps into his pants and boots.

Ready to go, he slides down the pole

Puts on his helmet and coat below.

Sirens blare, red lights glare

Fireman Small has no time to spare.

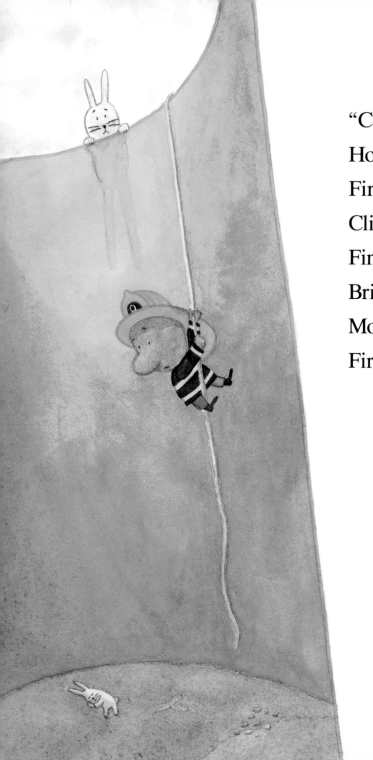

"Come quick!" Mother Rabbit cries,
Holding back the tears in her eyes.
Fireman Small peers in the well
Climbs down to where Little Bunny fell.
Finds Little Bunny asleep on the ground
Brings her back up, all safe and sound.
Mother Rabbit shouts: *"HOORAY!"*
Fireman Small drives back to the bay.

He pulls into station number nine.

Walks upstairs, one step at a time.

Closes the curtains, gets in bed

And pulls the covers over his head.

JING-A-LING-JING the telephone rings.

Bakery's on fire! Can't see a thing.

Quickly out of bed he scoots,
Jumps into his pants and boots.
Ready to go, he slides down the pole
Puts on his helmet and coat below.

Sirens cry, lights flashing by

Fireman Small sees smoke in the sky.

He hops down from behind the wheel

Jerks the fire hose off of the reel.

Breaks a window, knocks down the door

Puts out the fire at Bakerman's store.

Hippopotamus shouts: *"HOORAY!"*

Fireman Small has saved the day!

He pulls back into station number nine,
Walks upstairs one step at a time.

Closes the curtains, gets in bed
And pulls the covers over his head.

DING-A-DONG-DING the doorbell chimes!
Who would come calling at half past nine?

Fireman Small hurries downstairs,

Opens the door to see who's there . . .

It's his friends stopping by to say:

"Thank you for all your help today,

Thank you for making everything all right.

Now go to bed and turn out the light!"

Fireman Small waves goodbye,

Climbs back upstairs, rubbing his eye.

Stretches and yawns . . . crawls into bed . . .

And pulls the covers over his head.

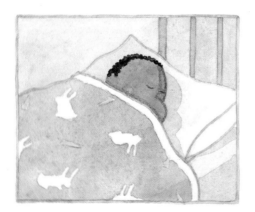